A Lucky Charm

ADAPTED BY BOB READ
FROM FRANCIS GREIG'S ORIGINAL STORY

Published in association with The Basic Skills Agency

Hodder & Stoughton

A MEMBER OF THE HODDER HEADLINE GROUP

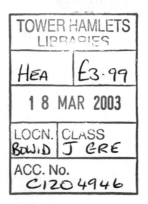
Order queries: Please contact Bookpoint Ltd, 39 Milton Park, Abingdon, Oxon OX14 4TD. Telephone: (44) 01235 400414. Fax: (44) 01235 400454. Lines are open from 9 am - 6 pm Monday to Saturday, with a 24-hour message answering service. Email address: orders@bookpoint.co.uk

British Library Cataloguing in Publication Data
A catalogue record for this title is available from The British Library

ISBN 0 340 59031 9

First published 1993
New edition 1996
Impression number   15 14 13 12 11 10 9
Year   2004 2003 2002 2001 2000 1999

A Lucky Charm is adapted by Bob Read from the original story, *The Hitchhiker,* by Francis Greig, first published by Jonathan Cape Limited, 1981, copyright © Francis Greig 1981.
This adaptation copyright © Bob Read 1993

Copyright © 1993 Bob Read

Printed in Great Britain for Hodder & Stoughton Educational, a division of Hodder Headline Plc, 338, Euston Road, London NW1 3BH by Hobbs the Printers Ltd, Brunel Road, Totton, Hampshire SO40 3WX

1

Carol did not know if she would get to Liverpool Street station in time for the last train. She had worked very late that night. Carol worked in a big shop on Oxford Street.

They had been getting the shop ready for the Christmas rush. It had been fun putting up the Christmas trees and the lights, but she felt tired now. In fact, she knew she would be too tired to cook when she got home, so she had stopped for a pizza on the way to the tube station. They had been slow to serve her in the restaurant, and so she had had to eat up and leave quickly.

As she left the restaurant, it started to rain. She did not like to walk on her own through London late at night, so she took a taxi. She felt safe and dry inside the taxi. She told the driver, 'Liverpool Street, please.'

She looked at her watch. Would she make it to the station in time? Perhaps, perhaps not, but there was nothing she could do about it anyway. She always felt the same whenever she took a taxi. In one way she felt in charge, because she was paying the fare. In another way, she felt rather helpless, a victim of some sort and in the hands of a complete stranger.

She looked at her watch again. The train left in twenty minutes, and they were stuck near

Covent Garden. Still, if the traffic was not too bad, they would just about make it.

She settled back into a corner and looked out of the window. She liked to drive through the city in the rain. The road was wet and shiny and reflected the bright white lights of the cars and the coloured shop signs. For once, everything in the city looked clean and new, she thought. Carol listened to the sweep of the windscreen wipers and the rain on the roof of the taxi. She began to feel sleepy. It had been a long day. She would be glad to get home.

At the station she looked out at the people and taxis and buses everywhere. It was always like this at Liverpool Street station, she thought, car doors slamming, buses hooting, people shouting and pushing past each other. And always people dragging cases, looking tired and lost and worried, like refugees from a war. It was busy like this all the time, she thought. No wonder she and her husband Tom had kept their house in Suffolk instead of moving to London.

Carol paid the driver quickly and looked at her watch. She had one minute to get to the train. She rushed into the station. She knew where to go. She ran straight to platform number 6. She was in luck. It was still there.

2

As Carol got on the train, she was still feeling out of breath. She felt people look up from behind their newspapers as she walked along the compartment to find a seat.

Carol made this train journey home every evening. Normally she sat with friends who also travelled into London to work. Tonight she was late and alone and did not recognise any of the other passengers. She chose her seat carefully.

She found a space at a table with a woman sitting with a young child. The woman looked up and smiled as Carol sat down. 'Not a very nice night, is it?' the woman said.

'No. And it seems to be getting worse, I think,' Carol replied.

She settled into her seat by the window. The light of the compartment seemed to shut out the weather. Carol was glad she had driven down to the station in Ipswich that morning. Sometimes she took a bus, but that morning she had been late and had taken the car. She had left it in the station car-park.

Carol looked out of the window. The lights from the train windows fell on to the edges of dark wet fields and trees leaning in the wind and the rain.

Yes, Carol thought, she would be glad to get into her car on a night like this.

She turned her head away from the window and settled back into the seat. She felt her head touch the padded head-rest. As her eyes closed, Carol thought about her day at work, about Christmas and the lights, about the jokes people make about her name at this time of year ...... Suddenly she woke up with a jump. Someone was touching her hand. What time was it? Was she late up for work?

'We're in Ipswich, love. I'm sorry. I didn't know whether ... .' The woman with the child was standing in front of her, smiling.

'Oh ... yes ... thanks,' Carol said. She put a hand to her hair, then rubbed her eyes. Had she slept all the way from London? She stood up and made her way quickly to the door. She thought she was the last person to get off the train.

―――――――――――――

3

All at once, Carol found herself outside on the platform. After the warmth of the train, the cold wind and the driving rain came as a shock.
She hurried into the shelter of the empty ticket hall. The ticket window had a sign saying 'Closed'.
It looked as though everybody had gone home.

She stood for a moment and felt in her coat pocket for her car keys and some money. She could hear the London train pull away. Once the train had left, the station was very quiet. From outside she could hear the wind and rain blowing against the windows. She went to the pay-phone in the corner to tell her husband, Tom, that she was on her way home.

She picked up the phone. She went to put in 10p, but the phone would not take the money. She looked down. A message in black letters flashed on and off: '999 CALLS ONLY ... 999 CALLS ONLY ... 999 CALLS ONLY ...'

She suddenly felt all alone. The bright busy streets of London seemed a long way away now. Tom was still half an hour's drive away through the wind and the rain. She wouldn't stop and eat in London again after work, that was for certain. If she had caught the earlier train, she would have been back home hours ago ...

Still, I'll soon be home now, Carol thought.
She had just put up her umbrella, ready to run for
the car, when she thought she heard a noise coming
from the platform, like a heavy bag or case being
dragged along the floor.

She looked back quickly towards the dark platform,
but all she could hear was the rain outside.
It was probably just the wind blowing some wet
newspaper along the floor, she thought.
Come on, Carol, she said to herself, get out to the
car and drive home. She felt angry that she had
given herself a fright like that.

She hurried out of the station to the car-park.
Because she had been late that morning, she had had
to leave her Mini at the far end of the car-park.
It was just an area of waste ground really with no
street lights. There was no shelter or fencing.
It was still raining very hard. She decided to run to
her car, which stood all alone on the far side.

It was difficult to run in the wind and rain with the
umbrella, and it was slightly uphill as well.
Half-way across, the umbrella blew inside out and
Carol nearly fell over. She almost dropped the car
keys.

All of a sudden, she felt close to tears. This was
turning out to be a dreadful night. She decided to be
more careful and take her time. She decided to walk
the rest of the way. If she lost the keys, she thought,
she would never find them in the dark.

Just as she set off again, she thought she heard someone call her. Was it someone behind her or just a voice in the distance carried by the wind?
She felt her heart begin to race. Don't stop, Carol, or look round, she thought. Walk quickly. It's only a little bit further now.

But when she was close to the Mini, she could not stop herself from running the last few yards.
The car was ten years old and a bit rusty but, goodness, was she pleased to see the old thing!
In a second she had opened the door and jumped in.
Just then, she heard the voice again.

———————————————

4

After she had slammed the door, she snapped down the inside lock. Even then, she could not stop shaking. She was shaking so much she was unable to put the key in the ignition. Then after a moment, she thought, 'That was a woman's voice.'

She looked out through the windscreen down the slight hill towards the station. It was very dark around the car, but against the lights of the station yard Carol could make out a short dark figure just a few yards away. It looked like a thin woman in a raincoat. She wore a headscarf that blew in the wind. She was holding a handbag. She did not have an umbrella. She looked very wet.

Carol wound down the window. The rain blew in on her face. She shouted, 'Is anything the matter? Can I help you?'

From out of the darkness she heard the woman call back, 'I didn't mean to frighten you. I thought you were the taxi I ordered. I couldn't see any other cars around.'

The lady stopped for a moment. It was difficult to talk into the wind and the rain. After she had got her breath, she went on, 'Could you give me a lift into the town?'

Carol felt relieved. She reached over and unlocked the other door. She would be glad of the company on a night like this. The poor old dear must be absolutely drenched. And with the phone out of order she wouldn't have been able to call another taxi. She was stranded! She had probably felt more frightened even than Carol!

The woman got in. Carol could not really see her face because of her headscarf. Carol said something about the weather as she reached over to the glove compartment in front of the old woman. The light of the glove compartment came on as she opened the flap.

She was looking for the wooden clothes peg that she used to keep the choke open. She called it her lucky peg. Her friends used to laugh at her for having an old car that needed lucky charms to keep it going. She smiled at the thought of her friends' joke as she went to shut the little flap. As she did so, she happened to look down at the woman's hands. The smile froze on Carol's face. In the light of the glove compartment, she could see the back of the woman's hands. They were covered in thick dark hair.

Inside Carol's head her brain screamed, 'It's a man! My God, it's a man!'

5

Carol tried hard to stay calm. She needed time to think of a way to get this man out of the car.
She kept talking about the bad weather. She played with her seat belt and the rearview mirror.
She adjusted the rubber mat under her feet. Her left hand was so tense she could not let go of the wooden peg. Then she had an idea.

Carol kept hold of the peg and turned the ignition key. She knew it would not start. She tried to start the car four times. She sighed and said, 'It gets like this in the winter. It only needs a little bit of a push to jump start it. It's such a little car and we're on a bit of a hill here. Do you think you could ... ?'

It was a slim chance, but it worked. The dark figure got out and went round to the back of the car. At that moment Carol reached over to shut and lock the passenger door. In an instant she had pegged back the choke-rod and turned the key. The car roared into life. Within seconds she was in third gear and at the other end of the car-park. Just before she left the car-park she looked in the rearview mirror.
She could still see the dark figure at the far end.
Then the rain came down harder, and the figure was lost from view.

The car rushed on to the main road and headed into the town. Carol drove like crazy in the rain for two miles before she realised she hadn't switched on her headlights or her windscreen wipers.

6

Carol pulled off the road into a garage to phone Tom.
The garage forecourt was busy and floodlit.
It was almost midnight, but on the forecourt it was as
bright as day. Carol felt strange standing there, as if
she was on a stage. She couldn't believe what had
happened to her just ten minutes ago.
Everything seemed so normal here. People were
filling their cars up with petrol. A man was bending
down to check the tyres of his car.

Carol went in to the garage shop to find the phone.
Inside, a couple were looking at the shelves of
videos. From the radio behind the counter she could
hear Bing Crosby singing 'White Christmas'.
The young girl assistant was reading a paperback.

The assistant looked up and saw Carol was upset.
Her face was still very pale. Her hands were still
shaking. The assistant asked, 'Are you OK?
Have you been in an accident?' Carol said,
'No. I mean, yes. I'm OK. I'm all right, thank you.
Where is your phone?' The assistant told her the
nearest phone was outside the pub, just over the road.

Carol walked over to the pub. She looked up.
The rain had stopped at last, and the sky had cleared.
Carol rang home.

Tom picked the phone up at once and asked if she was all right. He had been very worried. She said, 'Yes. I'm fine ... '

Carol suddenly realised she could not tell him her story over the phone. She needed to talk to him face to face. 'Yes. I'm fine, Tom. The trains were all running late. You know what British Rail is like! I'll be home in half an hour and tell you all about it then.'

She felt calmer after the call to Tom, but she needed to think again about what had happened. She noticed that the pub was still open. They must have an extension, she thought. She went in and ordered a vodka and tonic. She sat down by the warm yellow light of the log-fire. From another room in the pub she could hear people singing 'Happy Birthday'. She began to relax.

Was I really in danger, Carol wondered.
Perhaps I just panicked. The old lady did nothing really except ask for a lift. Did I really see hair on her hands? Perhaps she just wore those mittens you can get with no fingers. It had been almost dark in the car, after all.

Carol finished her drink quickly. She suddenly understood what she had done. She had probably left an old lady stranded in the dark on that waste ground. Perhaps she was still standing there, cold and wet and frightened. Would she be OK?
It was too late to go back and find her now.
Tom was worried already, and she had driven a long

way from the station, but Carol felt she must let someone know. Then she remembered that her way home took her past the police station. She ran out to her car and drove straight to the police station.

———————

7

The police officer on duty listened to her story and took notes. When she had finished, he asked, 'Before we send a man down there, can you tell me again what this woman looked like?'

Carol said, 'Well, she was short and quite thin, with a headscarf that hid her face. She was wet, because she didn't have an umbrella. All she had with her was ... '

Suddenly Carol remembered. She dashed out to her car. She ran back into the police station with the woman's handbag. The woman had left it on the passenger's seat when she had got out to push the car. Carol was excited. She said, 'Perhaps there'll be something in here that will tell us more about her!'

The police officer took the black leather handbag and put it on the counter by the desk lamp. It had a metal clasp. He snapped open the clasp and held the bag open. Carol looked inside. She screamed and grabbed the police officer's arm.

The shaft of the axe had been cut short so that it would fit into the bag. It was the only thing in there. The cutting edge shone silver in the white lamp light.

<hr>